Printed in U.S.A.
First American Edition
2   3   4   5   6   7   8   9   10

Library of Congress
Cataloging-in-Publication Data

Vincent, Gabrielle.
[Ernest et Celestine au cirque. English]
Ernest and Celestine at the circus /
by Gabrielle Vincent.
p.   cm.
Translation of:
Ernest et Celestine au cirque.
Summary: Ernest and Celestine go
to the circus where Ernest was once
a clown and take part in the show.
ISBN 0-688-08684-5.
ISBN 0-688-08685-3 (lib. bdg.)
[1. Bears—Fiction.   2. Mice—Fiction.
3. Circus—Fiction.]   I. Title.
PZ7.V744Erf 1989
[E]—dc19   88-23220   CIP   AC

GABRIELLE VINCENT

Ernest and Celestine
at the Circus

GREENWILLOW BOOKS, NEW YORK

Oh Ernest, I am so bored. I don't have anything to do.

Stop whining, Celestine.
You know we're going to the circus later.
Must I drop everything? All right, come on.

Wait till you see what's in the trunk.

This costume once made me famous.

I can remember
doing this years ago.

It takes a while
to do it properly.

First the eyes.

Then the nose....

Done!

This hat was my
trademark when I was
Ernest the Clown.

You can be a clown too, Celestine.

Oh Ernest, I feel silly.

We're off to the circus, Celestine!

Not dressed like this, Ernest!

You'll see, Celestine, it will be all right.

I can't wait to show you everything.

Nothing has changed. It's all just as I remember!

Look, Celestine. My old friend Bolero is going to make his
hat disappear. He always does that at the end of his act.

He was great!

Now it's our turn!

No, no, Ernest, come back!

Grab him! But look. It's Ernest the Clown!
Tell Maurice to introduce him!

LADIES AND GENTLEMEN,

PRESENTING THE RETURN OF ERNEST THE CLOWN AND HIS HELPER, CELESTINE.

Bravo, Ernestine.

No, my name is Celestine.

Why don't you share the flowers with your fans, Celestine.

Hooray for Ernest and Celestine!

Please come back tomorrow, Ernest.
There will always be a place for you in our circus.

It really was fun, Ernest.
I like being a clown!

See you tomorrow, Bolero.

It was great to have you back, Ernest.
Just like old times.

Tomorrow we'll do our old routine—
and add a part for Celestine!

I never thought we'd end up in the circus, Ernest.
We've always been a good team, Celestine!